MY **LIFE** AS A **FAIRY TALE**

THE

SNOW MAN

SPECIAL CHARITY EDITION

This is a work of fiction. All the characters and events portrayed in this work are either fictitious or are used fictitiously.

THE SNOW MAN

Publised by Erinyes Publishing, LLC
Atlanta, GA 30364

www.erinyespublishing.com

Author image © 2017 by Giles McBee
Cover image © 2015 by Mickey Desai

ISBN: 978-0692502099

SPECIAL CHARITY EDITION

Printed in the United States of America

To Christy

You became fluent in the language of my mind in an instant, and then translated it for the rest of the world.

For this, I shall be forever in your debt.

CONTENTS

PREFACE

THE TRUTH BEHIND THE TOWERS

In the summer of 2014, my husband began serving a multi-year sentence with the Bureau of Prisons. He was yanked out of my life and those events formed the basis of my short story "My Life as a Fairy Tale: The Little Mermaid."

"The Snow Man" tells of what could have happened next.

My life has become one of hyper-vigilance—my brain always on alert, never fully relaxing, never fully resting, always wondering what horrible news the next phone call or letter might hold. I began to experience emotion as part of a duality, where the excitement over receiving a letter was always paired with dread at what horrible news it might contain.

If anyone had told me twenty years ago when I left high school that I would be spend my nights learning about the American prison system, not to mention doing whatever I could to help those contained within its walls, I would have laughingly dismissed the prediction, since I was sure that nothing like that would ever happen to me.

As is often the case with karmic hubris, it did happen to me.

My own Prince is locked within the prison system, but he is not there alone. There are other men and women—cut off from their families, desperate for the love, the contact, and the connections which we habitually take for granted.

No other event brought this into focus more sharply than a letter I received last year from one of my husband's friends, a letter which told of his visions of black bags in the basement of the prison—lined up and waiting for inmates to die.

"I know, without a doubt, that there is one down there with my name on it."

I now understand what it means to have lost all hope.

My heart breaks when I think of those who are paying for their crimes, but those who choose not to abandon them. The people who choose love over hatred—or worse, apathy— and for their trouble become bound to the prison system themselves—living in a perpetual state of fear mixed with anxiety and dread, with only a glimmer of hope to light the way.

These are the fathers, brothers, mothers, sisters, husbands, wives, and friends. I can offer no excuse for those who are serving their sentences, but I have found that the hubris inherent in the system we use to penalize our citizens is nearly Olympian in nature.

If we truly wish to help those who have faltered regain their step, we must walk *beside* them and be willing to help. We cannot pretend these people do not exist, for it will only wound them further. We must do more than simply speak of forgiveness; in the end, we must forgive.

Zachary A. Calais
Day 944 of The Interim

THE SNOW MAN

PART ONE
THE FALL

I AM FORTY YEARS OLD, and for the second time in a single year, I am preparing to move. Brown cardboard boxes—some packed full, others partially empty, and a few which contain only air—are scattered across the dark, polished concrete floor of my loft. A network of barely-navigable paths spreads throughout the one-room living space, allowing me access to the only three pieces of furniture I still possess: a desk, a couch and a bed.

I have also managed to keep clear a path which leads to one of the tall, many-paned windows on the north side of the room. During the days when this building was still a factory, these windows might have been opened for ventilation, but they are now welded shut. The glass simply provides a breathtaking tableau of the city of Alexandria, Louisiana, and would never again allow in the occasional rustle of a gentle breeze.

With June drawing to a close, however, there is not even a whisper of a hint of a breeze—gentle or otherwise—to be had.

It is not yet noon, and the temperature has passed the ninety-degree mark hours ago. As I stand and look through the tall window, I can see the air over the Red River shimmer, blurring the buildings on the northern bank with a roiling, undulating haze.

Yet, there is something more dreadful than the scorching heat: the invisible sticky, swamp-like humidity which seems to smear itself on your skin, hair, and clothes, rendering any attempt at formal wear or hair style futile. Despite my hometown of Atlanta's more northern latitude, I had long ago grown accustomed to this smothering type of humidity, making my adjustment here quicker than I had originally anticipated. One thing which I had not anticipated was the foul, lingering odor in the air: a more-than-faint acrid smell of burnt petroleum. These days, it seemed as if every lawn mower and automobile had both spontaneously and simultaneously overheated. Then again, one could not travel five miles in any direction without happening upon a refinery, either great or small.

I do not live in Louisiana because of its weather or its aroma. I live here because I promised to love someone—for better or for worse—forsaking all others, including myself.

Prince Charming is in a Tower, but not a "tower" in the literal sense—it is a prison where the government chooses to house those which had been found in violation of its laws, a zoo where the cages do not house lions, or tigers, or bears.

These cages hold men.

While Prince Charming is currently in the Tower on the Beautiful Mountain, he was originally taken into the Tower which stands in the tiny hamlet of Elmdingle, less than an hour away from where I now stand. The American South is freckled with hundreds of the blink-and-you-miss-it towns, and Elmdingle was no different. Its size, however, was not among the reasons which eventually led me to Alexandria. There was no shortage of available properties; on my first trip out here I had discovered a spacious four-bedroom ranch which abutted the Tower itself. But with each and every house which I view, each and every encounter with the locals seemed tainted with a silent prejudice woven into the very fabric of the community, an echo of a whisper which said simply that outsiders were not welcome here.

Having my husband imprisoned in the Tower brought with it enough of a stigma; I did not wish to compound the issue further by living where I was not wanted.

Instead, I chose to exchange my hometown of Atlanta for a temporary residence in Alexandria, swapping the lost continent for the lost library. I had no connections with this new city, either familial, social, or professional. This suited me perfectly. I quickly fell into a habitual existence blessed with anonymity instead of novelty, and during the seven months, three weeks, and two days which I have I lived here, I had managed to learn only one person's name: Marla, the letter carrier upon whose route my building sat.

I worked from home, and it was not long before our paths crossed in the lobby. I would be running out for food or some odd errand and she would be sorting the mail into the small brass boxes from which the residents would later retrieve it.

Having been raised in the South, I have always felt that everyone—including strangers—should be offered a vocalized greeting and soon, we struck up a casual acquaintanceship. I plucked her name from the plastic tag on her shirt and she lifted mine from the envelopes she would deliver. She had even come to my door a few times, when something required a signature or was too large to fit in the letterbox.

As it turns out, Marla was not native to Louisiana, but had chosen to remain here after finishing college in Baton Rouge. I will never forget the look of mock indignation on her face when I opened the door late one morning after she knocked. She was holding a large, thick envelope by the very tip of one corner, her arm fully extended out, as if the envelope was radioactive.

The return address said "Tulane University" and I could only assume that it was the materials I had requested online about a week prior. I took the package, thanked her, and started to close the door when she stopped me with her voice.

"What I want to know is this," she said. "Why Tulane?"

Marla and I had never moved past the casual acquaintance stage, but I knew that she could read the return address on Prince Charming's letters. She knew I received mountains of mail forwarded from my old address in Atlanta, and I had caught her several times glancing at my wedding band in a not-so-subtle manner. I chose to move forward under the assumption that she possessed most—if not all—of the proverbial puzzle pieces and had already accurately assembled it.

"I wanted to go back to school," I answered, voicing my intention for the first time to someone other than my cat. "I had looked at Tulane when I was in high school, but never applied."

Marla simply stared at me, and for some reason I felt I had given her an incorrect answer.

"Honey," she said, shifting her bag on her shoulder so it settled onto her hip. "I know you wanted to go to school, otherwise you wouldn't be getting mail from Tulane. I just wanted to know why you were going to drive all the way down to New Orleans when Louisiana State has a perfectly good campus right here in Alexandria."

Silence was my response.

"Unless," she said, her words becoming more dramatic as she continued. "Unless you're one of those UGA fans who are have so much team spirit they should have their head examined."

A chuckle caught in my throat, and then I laughed.

Granted, it sounded like a cough—my voice rough from lack of use. But soon I was cackling in earnest, the first smile in months forming on my face. Marla's eyebrow slowly began to rise until it looked as if it would become one with her hairline.

"Yep," she said. "That's it. You need to have your head examined."

I managed to tell her that while a trip to a therapist might be a touch overdue, the hilarity of her suggestion that I was a fan of the University of Georgia was the actual joke.

I had not, nor would I ever be, a Bulldog fan for one simple reason: my father had attended Georgia Tech. For in the South, college football allegiance is right behind church denomination in the pecking order of social importance.

Having heard my rationalization and understanding it immediately, Marla seemed satisfied that I was not in any immediate psychological danger. As I promised to look into LSU, she said goodbye and started walking down the hall as I turned and started to close the door. Her voice stopped me once more, the door mere inches from latching shut.

"It don't matter if you go to school full-time and work full-time," she called from some distance away. "You're still going be missing him somethin' awful."

I stood there frozen with shock and said nothing. To my surprise, Marla was very adept at working out puzzles, seeing the situation not only for what it was, but how it did and will affect me.

Soon, the sound of footsteps in the corridor assured me Marla was on her way and it would be several minutes more before I would allow the door to close and force myself back into my near-monastic daily routine.

There was an almost-tangible lack of shock when—a few days later—Marla delivered an orientation guide and course catalog for LSU, her smug smile silent, wide, and in my opinion, capable of producing light. I promised her that I would look through it, but the very next day she brought a letter to me from Charming which burned down all my hopes for Alexandria, be they educational or otherwise. He had written to let me know that he was being transferred to another facility and the circumstances under which this transfer became a necessity.

If asked at the onset of the service of his sentence, I would have wagered my net worth that Prince Charming would have been physically assaulted within his first year of confinement. What I did not expect was that this violence would come, not from one (or more) of the other inmates, but at the hands of one of the guards.

Officer Young may not have been planning on slamming

my husband against a cinder-block wall when he went to work that morning, but while Prince Charming sat in the Secure Housing Unit "learning his lesson", I began to pack up my loft and learned a lesson of my own.

Not all criminals in the Tower are there involuntarily; some of them get to go home to their families every night.

Marla's knock at my door snaps me out of my memories and back into the present. She is the only one who has ever stopped by my loft before, as I have gone out of my way to be aloof with my neighbors, preferring to stay behind my own closed door as much as possible.

"Just a sec," I shout, realizing that I am not only shirtless but barefoot as well. Other people might consider it socially acceptable to answer the door dressed this way—Prince Charming included—but the rules of decorum drilled into my head by my Mother would forever prevent me from doing so.

I heard her voice in my head, "That would be...common."

I snag a random red t-shirt from the top of an unsealed box as I pass by and step into a pair of flip-flops which have been my only footwear for several weeks. Pulling the shirt over my head, I quickly glance down my chest to make sure there are no obvious stains. Mildly surprised that this garment seems to be clean, I resume my trek to the door. This particular shirt is a souvenir from a trip to the beach just before Prince Charming was taken away, and while it once fit me snugly, I have lost so much weight that it now hangs off my shoulders, the seamed sides flapping as I walk. Perhaps it would be more appropriate if the shirt said Georgia Tent & Awning, rather than the Tybee Island Yacht Club.

Marla knocks again, more forcefully than before.

"I'm coming," I shout, forcing frustration into my voice, though none exists.

"Well, hurry the hell up," she says through the wooden door, "I ain't got time to be beating on this door all day." Marla's frustration is far from false, it would seem.

"Okay, okay." I reach the door and turn the knob, beginning to draw the door back. Before I can get it open more than two inches, a large white Priority Mail envelope is thrust through the gap, hovering in the air momentarily until I take it with one hand. Immediately I hear Marla's quickly receding footsteps in the corridor, and I stick my head out my door just in time to see her shuffle through the door at the end of the hall, turning once to throw a brilliant smile in my direction.

"Work now," she said. "Talk tomorrow."

And with that, she was gone.

I pull the tab on the cardboard envelope, unzipping a slit in the top. I quickly glance inside at its contents, noticing only a handful of envelopes inside. My old next-door neighbor collects what little mail is still delivered to Atlanta, and forwards it when he gets enough to justify the postage for the cardboard envelope. Seeing nothing overtly urgent, I set it on the corner of my desk and drop into my chair, my attention once again not the city's skyline, but back on the designs for some marketing material on which I have been working for nearly two weeks.

My employer had been quite happy to take advantage of the surge in creativity that came shortly after Prince Charming's imprisonment. I might have been incapable of showering or eating with any regularity during those early days, but what little barrier remained between my imagination and the products of my imagination evaporated completely. The quality of my work doubled, tripled, and then to my own surprise, continued to grow even further.

Since I telecommuted, the lack of regular baths and meals bothered no one and allowed me to focus on my work, providing a small outlet for the maelstrom of emotions which swirled inside me. Functionality eventually returned to me, my left and right brains re-balancing themselves to allow me to survive the long road which lay before me.

My friends have often said that my practice of staying in my loft for days, if not weeks on end, could not be considered healthy. While I was always grateful for their input, I would always assure them there was no cause for concern. In many ways, spending a lot of time alone can be deemed healthier than nearly constant social interaction.

For example, I suffered no stress caused by a daily commute, nor was I forced to eat at restaurants every day for lunch. I could exercise when I wished, fold laundry while on a conference call, complete household chores while uploading files, and more than once I completed a project while a movie played on the television that hung on the brick wall above my bed.

Regardless, nature always demands a balance.

If there was ever a significant snowfall in Alexandria, I would not receive a spontaneous day off from work since my "office" was fourteen steps from my bed. Sick days were graded on a sliding scale: was I well enough to work, but not talk on the phone? Could I sit at my desk the entire day, or did I need to drag the laptop into bed with me?

I found it odd when I realized that I was somewhat grateful that my solitude also allowed me to process one unavoidable, inescapable fact:

I may not be single, but I am alone.

Prince Charming is in prison, and no matter the desire of my heart or the longing of my soul, he will not magically appear at the end of the day, as if this nightmare was anything but real. More importantly, I am completely and utterly powerless to do anything except that which I promised to do: love, honor, and cherish. I am prevented by the government from including "to have and to hold" in that short list of effortless labors of love because I, currently, do not have him and therefore cannot hold him.

Some days, I idly wonder if it is possible to sue the government for alienation of affection. I always dismiss the thought, for while it might be amusing, it is nothing but a flight of fancy that leads to nowhere.

The sun slips lower along the left-hand side of the windows, and as it does every day at this time, the glare becomes too much for my eyes. During my entire occupancy in Alexandria, I never quite figured out how to arrange the L-shaped glass-and-steel desk so that the sun does not reflect off the desk or monitor, or both.

It is during these afternoon hours which I—more often than not—literally put pen to paper: sketches, notes for a project, or even a shopping list that I will—without fail—leave behind on my desk when I finally leave to go to the store.

The forgotten list does provide some entertainment

when I return home, laden with bags, to see how much of my original list I was able to remember. I have even gone as far as to refer to the whole process as Grocery Store Bingo.

It is amazing the games even the most depressed mind will play.

Today, when I stand up from my chair, I notice the packet on the edge of my desk, and picking it up, make my way over to the couch. I invert the package, the handful of envelopes within sliding out and then slightly scattering on the cushion. Sorting through the pile, I quickly realize it is mostly junk mail, along with one or two pieces of real mail. There is even a holiday card from my aunt and uncle in Tucson, although the more I think about it, I am more inclined to believe that the six-month delay was more likely a result of my uncle's forgetful nature than the tardiness of the U.S. Postal Service.

Over the past year, I have become quite good at mail. Then again, in the past twelve months, I sent more letters, notes, and packages than I did in the four decades preceding them.

I set aside the idiosyncratic image of my aunt and uncle in ugly wool sweaters posing with a Saguaro cactus strung with lights and continue to flip over envelopes, dismissing each of them in turn. The last letter in the pile is face up and as I move the letter from AT&T—specifically addressed to "Resident"—my eyes land on the plain, white, #10 envelope, with printed labels for both the delivery and return addresses.

Unlike the rest of the items now in the discard pile, this is a piece of mail with which I am quite familiar. I know that inside I would find one or more sheets of yellow lined paper— pulled from an ironically-named legal pad—filled with words written in ink. The whitewashed exterior is a dead giveaway as to the identity of the person who wrote it, for it is the stationery which is available to the men who are forced to live in the Tower.

While I found it odd that Prince Charming would have written me at our old address, my curiosity was quickly outpaced by my excitement. I loved getting letters from Charming and had been amazed at how his command of the English language—arguably one of the most difficult tongues to tame—had improved over the course of his imprisonment thus far. I pulled the envelope open and slid out the two white sheets, opening them quickly.

Something is wrong. My hands begin to shake.

Prince Charming's handwriting is quite unique; I have often likened his penmanship to that of a medical doctor in the throes of a grand mal seizure. This writing, however, is neat, orderly, evenly spaced, and in pencil, rather than Charming's preferred red pen. The pages are white and not yellow. There is not a single thing about this letter which originated from my husband.

I quickly flip over the forgotten envelope and examine the return address label in earnest. I immediately recognize the address of the Tower in Elmdingle and then I read the name above it.

Suddenly dizzy, I collapse onto the couch as my stomach lurches. I involuntarily begin to read the letter, seeing the words but not completely understanding them.

Hello,

I do not know how much Prince Charming spoke of me, if at all...

Yes, he spoke of you, several times. He spoke of you out of fear, out of panic. He spoke of you often when he was in the darkest of places.

Yes, Dutchman. I know exactly who you are.

For over three hundred days, Prince Charming has lived in a world which I will never see except through his eyes. He sends infrequent letters, makes semi-regular phone calls, and while we used to enjoy weekly face-to-face visits, those stopped months ago when he had to be transferred to a completely different facility for his safety. I will never wince when I hear the metallic slam of the doors, nor feel my skin prickle in the antibiotic chill of the air. I can hear the ever-present touch of despair in his voice when he calls, or merely scrawls words into a short note or letter. My entire youth may have taught me how it feels to be trapped in an environment—be it my home, my school, or my service in the Navy, whose dogma of conformity was the very antithesis of my innate spirit.

In comparison to the forced assimilation endured by Prince Charming, my life lesson paled so much in comparison that it seemed to fade from existence entirely. Forcing Prince Charming to toe whatever line happens to be drawn that particular day is the psychological equivalent of trying to capture a supernova in a snowflake.

Once his freedom was stripped away and he was safely held within the Elmdingle Tower's walls, those in control continued their quest to strip-mine his core personality. For over a year before his confinement, Prince Charming had found the strength to face the demon which plagues his mind. Where most people simply have "ups" and "downs", his manic-depressive mentality would cause his emotions to soar to the heights of the Himalayan mountains, and then subsequently plunge to the depths of the Marianas Trench, the cycle repeating again and again, over and over, never to stop as long as he lived.

I had borne witness to some of his more apocalyptic episodes, and while fear would sometimes seize my heart, the undercurrent of my love for him would never waver. It was our love from which he would draw the energy necessary to heal himself after emerging from the emotional extremes, and while we both knew the cycle would never end, bearing the burden together seemed to make it easier on us both.

The fact that I would become someone else's anchor in life shocked me to the core.

After finally learning the name of this foe, Prince Charming chose an offensive attack rather than a passive defense: partnering with physicians, learning about his condition, and taking his medicine with an alarming regularity that I had never before beheld in my beloved.

We had been reassured that his treatment should, could, and would continue once the service of his sentence began. We were shocked when those charged with his care almost completely destroyed any progress he had made. With the stroke of a pen, they chose to deny him the medicine which was required in order to preserve the sanctuary of his mind.

Even today, I do not comprehend how a medical doctor can glean enough information through a video conference to provide the clinical basis to support reversing such a serious diagnosis. Nor do I understand how she possessed the audacity to note in his chart that he had been "cured" from a disease that had plagued Western medicine for centuries. I did feel, however, that if someone is actually as Hippocratically-gifted as this woman found herself to be, she should instantly qualify for the Nobel Prize in Medicine.

It would take three phone calls to Stockholm before I learned that I could not nominate her for that particular honor.

I finish the Dutchman's letter, releasing a breath which I did not realize I was holding. I fold it back into thirds, tuck it in the envelope, and set it on the cushion next to me—face up—the Dutchman's name clearly visible.

I sit and stare into space, the Dutchman's words instantly stamped in my memory, purely out of reflex rather than desire.

I do not move.

I do not speak.

My near-eidetic memory allows me to permanently store every word scratched onto those pages, but there is one sentence which jumps to the very forefront of my conscious mind:

I love him. Present tense.

Did the Dutchman think me such a fool that I could not tell the difference between present and past tense in the written word? While his command of the language was far from masterful, he managed to succeed in communicating his point well enough.

He was in love with the man that I had married, and for reasons that I could not fathom, he felt I needed to be aware of this fact. Part of me wanted to give over to fiery fury and tear the letter into a thousand pieces, while another part—a colder, more sadistic part—wanted to pen the Dutchman a note on my best stationery, detailing the myriad of ways I would one day enjoy Prince Charming's affections while he continued his cloistered existence in the Tower.

Fortunately for the Dutchman, my best stationery was packed away in a box in a storage unit in Atlanta.

I returned to the Dutchman's words and the true purpose of his letter:his concern about Prince Charming's health and welfare in the new Tower.

I was the only person on Earth who could give him any assurance at all.I knew in that very moment the Dutchman would go to his grave never knowing what happened to Prince Charming once he was taken from the tiny hamlet of Elmdingle and consigned to the Tower on the Beautiful Mountain.

The sun is completely gone from the windows when another knock on my door startles me from my meditation.

Who the hell can that be? The only person who has ever knocked on my door was Marla and she has already come and gone today.

Shaking off the Dutchman's words, I stand and wind my way over to the door, opening it without looking through the peephole. When I see the person standing on the other side, I am stunned into silence for the second time today.

It is my Mother.

I really should have looked through the peephole.

PART TWO
THE FREEZE

"Aren't you going to invite me in?"

Her surprise appearance at my door has caught me off guard, and I realize that I had yet to speak. I silently step back, and she takes two full steps inside before stopping, unsure of where to go.

"There are boxes... everywhere," she says, a slight sense of disapproval in her voice.

"I'm packing," I say simply, shutting the door. "Just follow the path."

"It would appear I that I don't have much of a choice," she says, turning away from me and stepping gingerly along the cleared concrete floor in the general direction of the couch. She clutches her purse to her chest and seems overly preoccupied with her balance. For a fleeting moment, I conjure an image where the cardboard boxes are replaced with lava pits, but I have the good sense to stifle the chuckle that rises in my chest.

While in recent years I have chosen to nurture my creativity instead of my intellect, it did not mean that I had spontaneously become a complete idiot.

Reaching the couch, she perches on its edge, her back ram-rod straight, her purse still in her lap. I already know she will not be staying here for very long. She never stays in my home for very long, regardless of its location, space, neighborhood, cost or general livability. It could only be my tangential relationship with day-to-day chores which makes her uneasy, but there are days when I honestly believe she is afraid that whatever infused my existence with life and shattered my self-imposed structure might actually be contagious.

"I'm in Baton Rouge for a conference this week and thought I would surprise you and take you out for dinner." This is the first I've heard of her trip—it had been longer than usual since our last conversation, not that we spoke with any regularity. She pops up from the couch as if the red fabric had bitten her. "Shall we? There's a steak place not far from here that has amazing reviews on Yelp."

Mother is anxious to leave and I know instinctively that there is more behind the façade of a mother-son steak dinner than a happy coincidence. In fact, my mind is so busy running through all the different scenarios that I offer no resistance and accept her invitation. I know I need to wash the sticky film of sweat off my body and I know that she would want me to change clothes. While I might not have an issue attending a royal wedding in a t-shirt and gym shorts, my Mother would settle for nothing less than long pants and a shirt which possessed a collar, preferably in tones which were muted and subtle.

I quickly showered and changed, emerging from the

steamy bathroom to see her still standing at the edge of the couch, her phone to her ear, wrapping up a conversation with someone. Noticing my readiness, she quickly ends the call, drops her phone in her purse and smiles at me.

"Much better," she says, beaming. "You can never go wrong with a golf shirt and khakis. Which club is it from?"

"Saint Andrew's," I reply as we step into the hall. I lock the door and begin making my way down the passageway toward the stairs.

"Really? Where did that come from?"

"The pro shop," I say flatly, and can hear her step falter behind me. I am grateful she cannot see the wry grin on my face. I decide to let her wonder whether or not I managed to pull off a trip to Scotland in the flurry of the past year.

We walk downstairs in silence, and when we reach the parking lot in front of my building, she insists on driving. She glares at my car as we pass, and for a moment, I am confused; it was as if the automobile was in some way responsible for my departure from my hometown. While it may have been the vehicle which carried me away from Atlanta, I was the one behind the wheel.

Very little time passes between leaving my building and arriving at the restaurant, although I am convinced this is less a function of distance and more a result of speed. As an experienced passenger in Mother's car, I often wondered if she did, in fact, have a cinder block wedged on top of the accelerator.

"Did you know that Baton Rouge means 'red stick'?" she asks, seeking solace in the safety of small talk.

"Yes," I reply.

"You did?"

"Yes, Mother," I sigh. "I speak French."

"I think I had forgotten that. I knew you spoke another language, but I honestly thought it was Spanish."

"That one too," I say, my tone banal. I hated small talk, but the niceties must be observed.

"Are you sure?"

"Sí."

We sat in silence as she careened around another corner ten miles an hour faster than she should have. I am reminded of Disney's Cruella de Vil and how she wielded her car as a weapon and this time I am unable to stop the small bubble of laughter which escapes from my mouth.

"What's so funny?"

"Nada," I respond, and realize I am now in danger of descending into a full-fledged giggling fit. I know it is merely my fear manifesting itself, but I am almost unable to control it.

"Well, you need to get control of nada," she says with a slight edge to her voice. "It looks like we're almost there."

My humor disappears from existence as I see the restaurant's sign glowing in the darkness ahead. I only hope they have a decent wine list.

Once we are safely seated at a square, white-clothed table in a quiet corner, I discover that not only do they have a decent wine list, but also have a particular pinot noir of which

I am quite fond. I hold the glass in my hand, slightly swirling it, my eyes fixed on the sheeting action as Mother looks over the menu in her usual manner—top to bottom, left to right. My choice had been made before we left my loft; I am somewhat of a purist when it comes to beef and my order had hardly varied over the years.

"You're staring," she says, her eyes never leaving the non-steak entrées. "Is something wrong?"

"Just waiting for the Four Horsemen," I state as casually as an apocalyptic reference would allow. "You did say that this place had amazing reviews on Yelp. I figured it must be the end of the world if you're going off reviews posted on a website. You're not the most technically-inclined person on the planet. After all, your VCR did blink twelve o'clock for nineteen years."

"Someone at the conference suggested it, and when I asked if it was good or not, they said it had amazing reviews. Then again, given where you chose to move, it's not like we had a lot of options."

She lets the disdain from her statement hang in the air as she swings her ice-blue eyes to me, fixing me with a look in which I can see the molten mass of a mother's love barely restrained by a thin shell of control. In an instant I know why she is here, and in the back of my mind, I can hear the telltale snap of the trap closing. She drove all the way here for one purpose: to convince me to move back "home."

"So tell me," she says, her gentle tone flawlessly forced. "Do you still think that moving all the way out here was such a wonderful idea?"

First that letter and now this, I think as I down what remains of my wine in a single gulp and setting the empty glass on the table.

Let the games begin.

Dinner is a riotous affair, and by "riotous", I mean I am already past the point at which I would happily use tear gas to bring it to an end.

Unfortunately, our salads have only just arrived.

While my Mother did not share my personal preference for red meat, her choice of venue serves two purposes. First, having one of my favorite foods should put me at ease, and secondly—and more importantly—the public setting would ensure that our exchange, which may at times become heated and barbed, would never escalate to the point of a public spectacle.

This is not the first time she has employed this particular tactic. She first used it when I was a junior at Wormwood Academy and was suspected of perpetrating a string of practical jokes on the school. Despite the school being unable to find proof of any wrongdoing on my part, I was still surprised when Mother had taken me out to dinner at Shoney's on Main Street. This was not a meal to celebrate being found "not guilty." She wanted me to know that she knew without a doubt that I was the culprit, and if I felt I was getting away with anything scot-free, I was only fooling myself.

"'Not guilty' is not the same thing as 'innocent'," she said that night.

From that point forward I would loathe the dinners at which we were the only attendants.

"I asked you a question," she states, her voice returning me to the present.

Part of me—the larger part, actually—does not wish to engage her, but the game has already been set in motion. All that remains is to let it play out and hope that tonight would mark the first time in which the outcome would be miraculously different than each and every other time which had come before.

"Yes," I say.

She opens her mouth to no doubt clarify her point further, but I interrupt her.

"To everything," I snap, my inflection harsher than I intend it to be. "'Yes' to moving out here, and 'yes' to acknowledge that you had asked me a question."

I am slightly ashamed at the arrogance in my tone, but I am careful not to let it show through my façade. Instead, I pick up my glass, not because I am thirsty, but simply because I want something in my hands. I fidget constantly, but when I become agitated and defensive, the involuntary movements increase tenfold. To be fair, Mother is one of the few people who can engender such a reaction in me anymore. The woman knows how to push every single one of my buttons; after all, she did install them.

"And now you're going to move." Her words emphasized and dramatic. After a longer-than-appropriate pause, she adds simply: "Again."

I stare at her a moment. When I speak, only a single word falls from my mouth.

"Yes."

In turn, she stares stone-faced at me for a moment, then

she begins to dress her salad, allowing me time to gather my thoughts. Unfortunately, once gathered, I find that my thoughts keep returning to the Dutchman and his letter.

I spear the lettuce in my salad with a touch more force than necessary as I think more about this stranger and what Prince Charming has said of him.

After Prince Charming's incarceration, I stayed in Atlanta for a while making ready for the move. It took quite some time to get everything organized and packed away so I could leave, unburdened by the flotsam and jetsam which we had accumulated as part of our normal, everyday lives.

Letters from Prince Charming would arrive regularly, if not frequently during the early days of our separation. He wrote of his life in the Tower, and the worries and fears with which he lived every day. He wrote of the multiplication of mania and deepening of depression, the former actually becoming evident by the increasing shakiness of his penmanship.

He wrote of those with whom he had chosen to associate: the Trickster, the Duke, the Sage and the Mister. These so-called "friends" helped him through his withdrawal from his medication and tried their best to help him adjust to the new life he must now lead. Some of them had chosen to write me directly, and—knowing that they were starved for any type of contact from the outside—I happily replied.

I may not have known what it was like to be in prison, but I knew what it was like to be alone.

I would soon learn of the Duke's dysphoria, the Trickster's

tantrums, the Mister's madness, and the Sage's sanctuary. In their own way, they brought Prince Charming a sliver of his former life, and while he did not have enough to make it whole again, he possessed just enough to create the illusion of happiness. That—at least for the time being—would be good enough.

The Dutchman, however, was not interested in helping Prince Charming, for the Dutchman only believed in helping himself. Through Charming's letters I would hear about the predatory advances which were made, and during phone calls my Prince's voice showed exactly how wearisome Charming was becoming with the Dutchman's longing glances from the distance which had been placed between them by Charming.

In the free world, the Dutchman's behavior would have been called "stalking." Inside the Tower, however, I believe it was referred to as "Tuesday."

There is a hard ping as the metal fork strikes the now-empty salad bowl. I am back in the present and my mother is casually eating her salad with one hand while holding her phone with the other. I set my fork down and move my plate to the side.

"Sorry," I say. "Apparently, I was hungrier than I thought."

"Apparently," she says, thumbing off her phone and setting it down on the table. "I must say it's odd to see you eat anything green without having to threaten you."

On this point, she is not mistaken. Throughout my entire life I have—with varying degrees of intensity—abhorred most if not all vegetables, their taste far too alkaline for my senses. As a child, I was often threatened with punishment if I did not consume the allotted portion placed on my plate by my parents. While this tactic had the desired effect in the short-term, I cannot help but feel that it did nothing but reinforce my hatred for leafy greens and legumes.

"How's Dad?" I ask, attempting to shift the focus of the conversation.

"He's doing good," she responded. "I asked him if he wanted to come with me this week, but he had already booked a couple of tee times. He said the golf courses down here weren't quite up to par."

We both roll our eyes at my father's play on words, and I'm sure we're sharing the same thought:

Amateur.

"Where is it you're moving to, again?"

And just like that, the focus of the conversation was squarely back on me.

"The Beautiful Mountain," I answer. "It's about three hours from here."

"Hm," she says. "Wouldn't it make more sense to stay where you are now? Three hours really isn't that far , and your loft isn't... horrible."

Coming from her, this was high praise indeed.

"Possibly," I concede. "It's not that far from Houston, so there will be more... stuff to do I guess." I am severely out of practice when it comes to these verbal tactics; I really only speak to Marla with any regularity. I occasionally speak to my cat Bastet, but she has yet to answer back.

"I'm not trying to be mean, but so what? From what I can tell, you never leave your loft as it is. Does it really matter if you live in a big city or a tiny, little town if you never set foot outside your door?"

My Mother is clearly not out of practice. I scramble to assemble something resembling a logical foundation to my argument.

"Well… I have to be there extremely early in the morning if I want to visit Prince Charming. It just makes sense to be closer."

"I thought visitation lasted into the middle of the afternoon," she countered. "Why do you have to be there so early?"

Something inside me snaps, and suddenly I am operating on instinct instead of conditioning.

"I just want to be closer to him" I say, my voice rising slightly in volume. Mother's eyes widen and her eyebrows arch, her silent suggestion demanding that I regain my composure. I obey, and my next statement—despite the vulnerability it exposes—is murmured so softly that I am almost whispering.

"When he's far away, it hurts."

Mother has the decency not to say anything.

Our entreés arrive, and we are silent for a few minutes as we begin to eat. I have always preferred my steaks the same way I prefer my wine—chewy and blood-red.

Mother returns to the safety of small talk, and begins to ask me questions about what it is like to visit Prince Charming in the Tower. For the first time, I cannot detect a shred judgment in her voice.

I explain that paying a visit to one of the Towers is a truly unique experience—one which most of the population will never have to endure. The Tower's primary concern is neither the convenience nor the comfort of the visitors, but the "protection" and custody of those who live there.

I think briefly how strange it is that we use the same word—custody—to describe both the imprisonment of criminals and the welfare of children. I set that irony aside for further reflection, preferably at a time when I'm not playing defense against my Mother on a mission.

I tell her about my very first trip to the Elmdingle Tower, shortly after Prince Charming had been taken away. I had yet to move from Atlanta, and wanted to scout the local real estate. The Dowager Queen—Charming's mother—and I traveled all day and all night from Atlanta one Friday. Fortunately, Charming's friend, the Sage, had provided us with detailed instructions on all the critical components of a successful visit: what time to arrive (five o'clock in the morning), where to line up (in a parking lot half a mile away), where to park (in a completely different parking lot adjacent to the Tower), what to bring (identification and coins for the vending machines), and, most importantly, what not to bring (anything else). A dress code would be strictly enforced, a fact which caused me to graciously endure lingerie shopping with my mother-in-law so she could purchase a brassiere without an underwire. Despite being a mild day in the middle of winter, we still stood in line in the second parking lot for almost four hours before being allowed inside.

After our identification was checked, we were led with the other eight members of our small group through a series of self-locking doors, the one behind us closing before the one before us could be opened. As we shuffled haltingly forward, I imagined that this must be what traffic in the Panama Canal must feel like. The simile soon soured when I was suddenly struck with exactly how apropos it was:

To those who chose to work in the Tower, the men who were forced to live there were nothing but cargo.

"So now you're picking up and moving to another state. Exactly how many times do you plan on going through with this?" she asked.

"As many times as it takes," I sigh. I really do not have the strength to explain my reasoning right now; the Dutchman's words are currently occupying a large portion of my brain and impeding my ability to answer my Mother's question. With his letter, the Dutchman instantly made me question every single thing I was doing to support Prince Charming.

"That is a plan which hardly breeds stability," she says in a not-so-subtle manner, though the timbre of her voice is pitched under her breath. "How does that Carole King song go? Where he leads, you will follow?"

"He's not exactly leading," I say, then stop short.

Dammit, I thought. *I walked right into that one.*

"I know that. He has to go where they tell him to go." Despite the skill with which she pulls off 'smug', it is not, nor has it ever been, a good look on her.

"You, however, have choices. I still don't understand why you left Atlanta; you still have a home there."

Although my mind is still reeling from her logical snare, the word "home" pushes through the haze.

"No," I say quietly. "I don't."

Her eyes widen comically and her face flushes with anger.

"Don't tell me you were stupid enough to stop making payments on your house," she says, her eyes darting about as if a representative of my mortgage company was coincidentally in the restaurant, and would happily verify my payment history.

"No," I say again. "I've been making the payments. I just don't have a home in Atlanta anymore."

"But you still own your house, right?" There is desperation in her tone; she is genuinely frightened that I have gone and screwed up something so badly that she will need to swoop in and rescue me.

"Yes," I say. "Think of it this way: I am a homeless house-owner."

A breath explodes out of her mouth as relief flickers over her face. The white skin over her knuckles fades back to its normal fleshy tone as her hands unclench, the napkin she was holding now mostly, if not permanently, creased.

Mother sets her fork down, her chicken half done, signaling the midpoint of the meal. It was time for the true discussion to occur, each of us sated by the meal thus far, and the remainders of adequate portions to be taken home should they sit untouched for the duration.

"Why don't you tell me more about how you visit him in prison," she asks. Her prompting might seem innocent on the surface, but I could smell a horse, specifically, a Trojan one.

"Well, all in all, they're not that... terrible," I begin, but she cuts me off.

"I mean... What would it be like if I went to visit him?"

I do not even try to conceal a grin as I answer.

"Short-lived. He would probably drop dead of shock if he heard you were waiting to visit."

Mother's jaw sets, and immediately I know I have struck a nerve. An emotion I cannot decipher flashes across her face before the well-trained mask slides back into place. I feel something akin to guilt welling up inside me, though I do not know its cause. I either feel sorry for wounding my Mother, or I feel sorry because I know that Prince Charming is so starved for human contact that he would welcome any visitor— even the icy presence of his own mother-in-law—gladly and happily, and probably without question.

I realize that I am a complete and utter asshole.

"Try again," states Mother, matter-of-factly, the hard line of her mouth betraying nothing. I fumble with my fork momentarily, then give up and simply place my hands in my lap.

"It would be just like if I went to visit him," I begin. Suddenly, she is looking at her plate, then her glass, then the waitress, then the decor on the walls... everywhere but at me.

A pit begins to form in my stomach; I know what's coming, and have little time to stop it.

"Well, I seriously doubt that. Aren't you two allowed..."

My hand flies up of its own accord, gratefully halting my mother's statement. I do not believe there are enough therapists in the entire State of Louisiana to help me cope with the trauma of my mother asking about a conjugal visit.

"They don't allow that," I say, hopefully putting the topic to bed.

"Well, on *The Good Wife*..." she begins.

"That's television; that's not real life, Mother," I interrupt her tersely. This is not the first time I have had to correct a misconception or two about what is real and what is fiction. "I've been meaning to ask you: how are you liking *Orange is the New Black*?"

She silently stares and steams at me. One of the perks of a near-eidetic memory is my ability to pluck words verbatim from weeks, months, years, or decades from my past. Mother absolutely abhors it when I do this. The maneuver works; she begins to move more and more off her guard, allowing me to assume a more offensive position rather than worrying about playing defense all the time.

"You usually stand in line for hours. You are surrounded by every type of person imaginable—from the humble, older couple who drove five hours just to be able to see their son for half that time, to the various wives or girlfriends who think they're doing the inmate and, quite possibly the rest of the world, a favor simply by being there. You can't even have your cell phone with you while you're standing in line, or a book, or... anything. Everyone tries to make small talk, but not a lot of people have the skills needed for a lengthy verbal exchange."

"I hope you're not one of... them," she interjects, with only the slightest emphasis on the last word. I do not know if she is referring to incapable of conversation, or if she believes I act like the other self-entitled spouses.

I raise an eyebrow in a subtle salute.

"Of course not," I assure her. "You taught me better."

"At least I got one thing right," she says, picking up her knife and returning to her meal. This subtle action means only one thing: she wants to listen, not talk. I oblige her.

"Nearly everyone will talk about what they are missing that day, or what they're giving up to be there, depending on their own personal degree of narcissism. Then you get searched; it's a lot like the airport but a touch more thorough. I like to think of it as… I don't know… 'TSA-Plus'."

I add air-quotes for effect, although I doubt she can see them; her eyes are still on the plate.

"We can hug once when he comes in the room and once when we leave. The manual even states that a 'chaste kiss' is acceptable, but given the geography, we are too afraid to test the boundaries of that particular rule."

Mother shifts in her chair uncomfortably—the subject of affectionate displays between me and members of the same gender have always been conspicuously avoided. There might as well be a sign that said 'HERE BE DRAGONS.'

"What happens then?" she asks, moving the conversation forward.

"You sit across from each other. You talk."

"That's all?"

"Yes, Mother," I say, "that's all. There's an amusing silence after about a quarter of an hour when you realize that you don't have to compress your conversation into fifteen minutes. I usually grab some junk food from the vending machines; Prince Charming has a notorious sweet tooth."

"How long do you get to stay?" she asks, as if this were an outing to an amusement park. In this case, however, my emotions are the only thing which resemble a roller coaster.

"It varies," I respond. "At first we would hold out until the very last minute, but once we hit a stride, we would sometimes end our visit early if they asked people to leave so they could allow other visitors into the room. Since I was living so close, Charming would feel bad for those people who drove hundreds of miles for just a single day."

Her eyes quickly pop up, confused. She is surprised by this fact.

"Surely, they don't drive hundreds of miles," she says, the question wrapped in the folds of a foregone conclusion.

I decide to adjust her conclusion.

"Mother, it was six hundred miles from my house to Elmdingle. That's why I moved. And to be honest, I really don't regret it at all."

"That's the price you pay, I guess," she says.

Capitulation with a touch of passive-aggression. It's a classic.

The more I reviewed our conversation in my head, excluding my jab about Prince Charming having a heart attack if she chose to visit him in prison, it was so rote we might have been reading from scripts.

"What I still don't understand is this," she continues, "and this could just be...me. Why would you want to go every weekend?"

Oddly, this used to be the easiest question I've ever had to answer since Prince Charming has been in the Tower, and while Mother has asked me the same question multiple times, she has always received the same answer. I go because I want to see my husband. I go because keeping in touch with the "outside world" is the only thing which seems to help, not only Prince Charming, but every other inmate in all the Towers throughout the land.

But today's answer is different. Today, I got a letter from a man who said he was in love with my husband.

I realize I have been staring into space for the last few minutes, and I decide to change up the play. I drop every mask and shield I have in place and allow her eyes to see the raw emotion in my own. When we connected, she dropped her fork, and sat back in her chair quickly, as if she had been pushed.

"I don't want him to forget me."

There it is: one of my deepest fears now exposed—in front of my most capable adversary, nonetheless.

Many outside observers simply assume that my Mother and I hate each other. This is not, nor has it ever been, the truth. Not once have our words or actions toward the other been borne from malice, despite how they may have been perceived as such. In fact, quite the opposite is true. We both are possessed by an innate desire for a relationship of some appreciable depth; what we lack is the capability.

Despite our outward resemblance and inward similarities, she and I were simply not wired properly for a traditional "Leave It To Beaver" existence. Over the years, she would hide me in obscurity and I would obscure her in the caricature of a Machiavellian ice queen. While this solution might be deemed unconscionable by "normal people", I am grateful to exist on the fringe where few people know of me. After all, I have been socially awkward almost my entire life, and the outskirts of society is a place that I could find comfort, if not total safety. Likewise, in my personal pantheon of goddesses, my Mother became Atropos, she who could never be swayed, the oldest of the Moirai: those three goddesses who held the fates of all mankind in their hands; goddesses so powerful that even the mighty Zeus was wise enough to fear them.

However, neither Mother's social circle nor the ancient Greek gods are here at the table, looking on as my single-largest vulnerability lay exposed. Mother's eyes quickly scanned my face, taking inventory. When she spoke next, her tone was soft and almost comforting.

Almost.

"I don't think he would ever forget you," she said. "If anything, I think he might be worried that you will forget him."

My breathing slows and I start to relax.

"Although," she says in the same gentle manner, "I'm not one hundred percent sure that forgetting him is a bad idea, at least for now."

Mother giveth, and Atropos taketh away.

I feel my body temperature increase, slightly at first, then growing exponentially hotter.

The anger which was building inside me must have been apparent in my face, because for the first time in my life, my Mother began to shrink away from me. Perhaps she remembered that the only other person to suggest that I set Prince Charming aside—even temporarily—wound up with a broken jaw.

My eyes bore directly into hers, and despite my anger, I held no intention of striking my own mother. To do so would be socially unacceptable.

I exhale a carefully-controlled breath and close my eyes for a moment. Like the manic depression which plagues my Prince, this discussion has a predictable, if unfortunate, cycle. It was long past the time I got off this damn merry-go-round.

I place my fork in the center of my plate and slip my steak knife into the gap between its center-most tines. I grab a quick sip of water and push my chair back from the table.

"Where do you think you're going?"

"Back to my place," I say, my tone forcedly casual. "I hope you enjoy the rest of your trip, and make it home safe. Tell Dad I said hello."

"Wait a minute! We are not through!" she says, her silverware clattering to her plate. Her eyes dart around the restaurant , unsure of what to do next.

I know now that changing the play is the right thing to do; sometimes in life, your only option is to call an audible.

"No, we're not through, but we are done for tonight." I could not afford to have both Atropos and the Dutchman inside my head together; my cranium would collapse beneath that burden.

"How are you going to get home?"

"The same way I got back the last time you and I got into a fight about my marriage," I say as I stand up. "Without you."

I ensure my back is ramrod straight and my shoulders are squared as I stalk away from her, my courage and resolve superficial at best. I do not even pause at the hostess stand, but instead walk through the door and into the parking lot. Fortunately, there was a bar next door where I could sit in smoke-filled, neon-lit anonymity, sipping a Scotch while waiting for a cab. Through the blinds on the bar's windows I see my Mother come out of the restaurant, phone to her ear, no doubt conversing with my father. She looks left, then right, then looks down as she ends the call, her eyes lingering on the phone for a long minute. Even from this distance I can see the bright reflection of tears in eyes which are the same color as my own, and my heart sinks as I watch her wipe them away with the back of her hand.

I know that she is smart enough to figure out where I am, but the woman who brought me into the world does what I imagine is the hardest thing for a mother to do: she climbs into her car and drives away, an aging Southern belle disappearing into the dark Louisiana night, leaving her child to deal, not only with the consequences of his choices, but the details of the decisions he would have to make for himself.

The taxi deposits me back in front of my building, and I waste no time in getting inside. Dinner with Mother has only served to increase my confusion and fear, these negative emotions having been placed in my head by the Dutchman and his wretched letter.

Why is this affecting me so badly? Even in my most fearful of moments, I can always draw strength from the bond which Charming and I share. Even now, I could still feel the strength I need so desperately from our connection, but the line was now clouded by static—static which has been placed there by a narcissistic sociopath whose only purpose was to possess Prince Charming for himself.

I slam the door behind me and lean back against the cool wood. The noise of my arrival prompts Bastet to slowly raise her gray, tabby head out of a partially-packed box on the floor. Sensing no immediate danger, she slowly lowers herself into her cardboard den, and I am reminded how I seem to be playing whack-a-mole constantly with that damn cat.

One of these days I fear I may accidentally seal her in one of the boxes and not discover my grave error until I have arrived at the Beautiful Mountain.

Thinking of Prince Charming's current Tower causes a geyser of memories to erupt in my mind, and I quickly cross the large space to my desk where the Dutchman's letter sits in the center of my blotter like an unexploded bomb: the innocuous white envelope harmless on the outside, yet containing enough ammunition to bring my world crashing down around me.

I snatch up the envelope and pull out the pages, quickly but carefully reading them once more, allowing more of his phrases and words to settle into my thoughts.

Prince Charming was...IS my best friend, and I miss him terribly. I'm worried beyond consoling and reassurance. How is he? How is he coping in his new place? Has he made any friends like me yet?

I pray to any deity that might be listening that Prince Charming has not met anyone like the Dutchman in the Tower on the Beautiful Mountain. Charming's correspondence has been somewhat scarce of late, and I am never sure of what constitutes friendship when one is confined in a Tower.

Prince Charming holds the answer to that question, and I am not entirely sure I want to ask him.

I angrily shove the Dutchman's letter back in its envelope, not caring that the corners are now bent, and throw it down on my desk. The slight buzz I felt from the Scotch is starting to wear off, and I am suddenly weary from a day full of more social interaction and human contact than I normally endure in a month.

If anyone is foolish enough to tell me right now that I should get out more, I would tell them to go to Hell in such a manner they would look forward to the trip.

I collapse, fully-dressed, onto the bed, and see Bastet slowly raise her head out of her box du jour. She either senses my distress, or is simply happy at my lack of movement, because she bounds from box to box until she lands on the bed. Climbing up onto my chest, she quickly settles down, sphinx-style, then rubs her face along my chin. She stares into my eyes for a long moment before turning her head to one side, her own eyes squeezing shut.

I know from experience that any movement on my part would result in her claws sinking into my skin, so I close my eyes too, and before long, drift off into sleep.

It may have been a noise that startled Bastet in the near-silent darkness, or it might have been her persistent yet simple sadism which causes her claws to extend into my skin only a few hours later. Not one to do anything by halves, she launches herself from my chest with the force of a Saturn V rocket at takeoff.

Needless to say, I am wide awake.

Part of me—a very, very small part—feels something akin to gratitude for being roused from slumber, despite Bastet's methodology. My restless dreams had starred Prince

Charming, as they do almost every night. In tonight's dream, however, I found myself in what I could only assume was the Tower with my Prince, my mind supplying the institutional backdrop that I had never seen. I was chasing him through a labyrinth of corridors and hallways, through doors and archways, but he always remained a couple of steps ahead of me, slightly out of reach. As soon as I would almost catch up to him, he would either turn a corner which had suddenly appeared, or quicken his pace until we were both running, always able to elude my desperate grasp. The chase wore on for what seemed like hours, until I rounded another cinder-block corner and saw him standing at the blind end of a dead-end corridor. As I approached, he turned to me, his eyes bright, his smile pure, and then he vanished into thin air, leaving me astonished and alone. I turned to see if he had simply jumped behind me, only to find myself face-to-face with a mob of faceless men in orange jumpsuits, the traits which would have made them unique washed away. A heartbeat later, I realized that they were slowly lurching toward me, and I backed up until I felt the ice-cold hardness of the wall behind me. The faceless mob continued their slow approach, the speed of their steps restrained by the confidence in knowing that their prey was trapped.

The more I think about my dream, the more I try to understand it, although I know the effort is futile. I can barely comprehend what Prince Charming endures when I am awake and functional; to expect more from my dreams would be a fallacy.

Without summons, the Dutchman appears in my now-conscious mind, and with him another phrase from his infernal letter:

Please just send word he is all right, and I will never bother you again.

I wonder if the Dutchman understands that while his words might sound like simply a request to him, to me they carry the full weight of a threat.

I bolt upright, and quickly glance at my bedside clock; it is only two a.m. Despite the darkness that drops through the huge windows, I already feel a full day's energy surging through my body. It is not uncommon for me to rise before my alarm sounds at six a.m.; my brain manages to maintain a constant state of activity which often denies me a full night's rest. Tonight is more of the rule, rather than the exception.

I swing my legs over the bed and as I stand up, I can still feeling the pain in my chest where the cat used me as a springboard. Beneath it, I feel the pain in my heart where the Dutchman's silent words are running amok.

I plod over to the corner of the loft where the kitchen is located, and stand in front of the coffee maker. While I am internally resigned to yet another early morning of activity before dawn, if I make coffee, I know that I will feel as if I have surrendered to the fact that I will not return to bed until tonight.

I look back at my bed, and it looks as if I have already made it, just as I do every morning. I return to the task at hand, scooping the ground coffee into the filter basket, and use three bottles of purified water to fill the reservoir. I press the button that was previously labeled On/Off on the front of the machine, the text having worn off months ago due to daily use. It was the only flaw in the machine which still worked fine.

While the machine gurgles and begins to drip the steaming brown liquid into the carafe, I stare the green LCD numbers on the front of the coffee maker which display the time. When Prince Charming was first imprisoned, we found ourselves in two separate time zones, a single hour separating our existences. I picked up the habit of automatically calculating what time it was for him every time I saw a clock.

Now, our geography has changed. Now, I calculate what time I would arrive if I chose to travel the distance between us.

This morning's result—five a.m.— resonates with me mostly because it is the time I would usually arrive when visiting the Tower. I pull a disposable coffee cup and a lid out of the cupboard, followed by a plastic spoon from the drawer immediately below. I gave up metal utensils and stoneware cups when I moved to Louisiana; it made no sense to use permanent things in a place which was temporary.

My morning joe prepared, I take the cup and walk back to the couch, thumbing the switch on the side of the TV along the way. I am greeted by the sounds of an early-morning news broadcast, two highly polished news anchors with brilliant white smiles informing me of events that would never have made the cut during the normal newscast. Sipping my coffee, I settle on the couch and notice that Bastet is nowhere to be found. My chest still resonates a dull ache, and it is probably best that she remain invisible for the time being.

As the woman on the TV talks about a local library's summer reading program for the children of the town, I find myself tuning her out so I run through the Dutchman's words one more time in my head. The now familiar anger flares again, and I know that I will not get any answers from the overly-coiffed woman on the screen.

There is only one place I can get the answers I need, and, if I leave right now, I would arrive in time to be one of the first people admitted to the visiting room. Today is not just another day for me, with work and whatever else waiting for me at my desk.

Today is Saturday.

I spring from the couch, pick up my keys and my phone, and leave my loft, locking the door behind me. Soon enough, my white Mustang was pulling out of the parking lot, turning south for the journey to the Beautiful Mountain.

It turns out that sleeping fully-clothed and always making your coffee "to-go" occasionally yields a hidden benefit; the time between my decision to demand answers from Prince Charming and my departure from my loft was less than three minutes.

Part Three
The Thaw

The route to the Beautiful Mountain, ironically, requires me to pass through the sleepy little town of Elmdingle, and in the pre-dawn hours, the streets and shops stand as deserted as they do in the middle of the day. The parking lot of the largest building in town—a Walmart, naturally—is empty except for a few stray shopping carts, abandoned by the workers before they went home last night.

Trees begin to crowd the road on both sides as I pass through the southern edge of town, their slender trunks made white by my headlights before they slide by me and back into the darkness again. There are no streetlights in this forest primeval, and I always feel a sense of claustrophobia as I ride this road which shoots straight through woods. I remember hearing fairy tales as a boy and always wondered why everyone thought the forest so scary; there was nothing to fear in the sculpted suburban landscape of my youth.

It took precisely one drive through these particular woods at night for me to completely and permanently adjust my perspective.

I hate making this drive on my own, and today more than ever, I wish to talk to someone. I glance at the clock - only an hour has passed since I awoke. There is only one person who is not only awake at this hour, but would also answer her phone if it rang. The fact that she is an expert in matters of not only the heart in general, but my heart specifically: Aphrodite.

I tap the quick-dial icon on the screen of my phone, then set the call on speaker-phone. I wedge the brick-like device into a cradle attached to the dashboard, so I can use both hands to drive.

I'm not out of the woods yet.

Aphrodite answers after only two rings, and I can distinctly hear voices and the thump of music in the background.

"Did you go to bed with a busy brain again?" she asks instead of saying "hello" like a normal person. Then again, if she were normal, we probably would not be as close as we were.

"Always," I say. "Are you still at the bar?"

"Thankfully, no; tonight was a complete cluster. We're back at my place just starting to unwind a little bit."

In a gap between corporate jobs, Aphrodite had taken to tending bar in a taphouse less than a mile from her apartment. It was not uncommon for some of the staff—or the occasional patron—to be invited back to her place after closing, where they would usually stay up until at least dawn.

Personally, I do not envy her for this behavior; there was a time when Artemis and I did the exact same thing. Aphrodite was almost a decade younger than Artemis and myself, and I try not to get jealous of the energy of youth: to do so would remind me of exactly how little youth remained in me.

"Oh, okay...um, we can talk later," I say, feeling guilty for disrupting the festivities. "No big deal."

"No, no, no, my dear," she says, her tone deceptively gentle and warm. "We can talk now. Hold please."

I hear the rustle of fabric against the phone, followed by Aphrodite's muffled voice instructing her guests on how to behave while she steps outside for what could very well be a long conversation. Soon enough, the pressure is removed from the phone, and in an instant I know what Aphrodite had done in lieu of using the mute button: she simply shoved the phone in her bra.

Did I just get to second base?

"Okay, I'm back," she says. "What's up?"

"Not much," I say. "Like I said, I'm just calling to chat."

"Bullshit. It's three in the morning and you're already driving somewhere. Where ya' goin', sweetheart?"

I could easily stall for a few minutes while I collect my thoughts; I could probably get away with it for ten full minutes before Aphrodite throws what remains of decorum aside, and begins to drill me with questions to which I would have to provide answers—answers that I was unsure that I possessed.

I choose to skip any pretense of delay, and begin to relate the events of the past twenty-four hours. I go back to yesterday's beginning, from the sun, the heat, and the letter. I weave in the details and my feelings about what happened at dinner with my Mother, and open up about not only where I was headed, but the emotion and fear which spurred my near-midnight ride to the Beautiful Mountain.

Contrary to what she often allows other people to believe, Aphrodite's true talent is not held in her bountiful bosom; it is her ability to silently draw from anyone the secretive truth that we all carry with us, yet rarely admit to anyone else—including ourselves. Her ability to tolerate bullshit is naturally low, and with me it is removed completely.

"Wow," she says, and I cannot tell if she is being sarcastic or serious. "Artemis was right, you are an adorable idiot."

This is one of the very few times that I feel anything resembling regret about hosting that small, post-nuptial gathering in our home, where my closest friends all met for the very first time. Now, they talked amongst themselves.

"I beg your pardon?" I force astonishment into my words, though to be truthful, none exists.

"You heard me," she said, with a touch more bite than I felt was absolutely necessary. "It's the middle of the night..."

"It's morning," I interject.

Aphrodite was Not Having It.

"It's night for normal people. You know what? I don't give a damn. It's pitch black outside, and you've spontaneously decided to jump in the car and drive for three hours so you can confront your husband because—and let me make sure

I'm getting this right—some psycho who was locked up with Prince Charming wrote you a letter?"

While her words may sound like a question, deep down I know it is rhetorical at best. I open my mouth to say something, but she had already built up momentum.

"Sure," she continued, "the letter was an atrocity. Honestly, I'm even a little pissed off about it. Sure, it was inappropriate. And yes, it hurt your feelings, but now you're just wallowing in it, and you can't even see the big picture anymore. And that, my dear, is what makes you an adorable idiot."

I suddenly found myself fondly remembering and slightly wanting of the more subdued approach which Artemis typically used when pointing out my flaws. Although to be fair, both Artemis and Aphrodite wound just as deeply as the other.

"Are you still there?" she asks. "Hello?"

"Yes, I'm—" I begin, but am once again cut off.

"If you just slowed down and thought about it for thirty seconds, you will see that there is nothing for you to worry about. Didn't Prince Charming tell you everything last fall when the stalking started?

"Yes, but..."

"Hasn't Prince Charming done sweet little things for you this whole time, leveraging every single inside joke the two of you have—which is a lot, by the way—to make sure that your marriage got the attention it deserved?"

"Well, yes, but..."

"Didn't Prince Charming send you a teddy bear for Valentine's Day because he knew how hard the holiday was going to be on you, and he wanted you to have something to just fucking hold on to?"

"Well, yeah, but how do you know about..."

For once we are both silent. I think about the package Marla had delivered back in February, which had lacked a return address. I remember the shock and joy I had felt when I pulled the traditional brown, fuzzy teddy bear from the box, with red hearts on its paws. I remember crying when I saw that the bear was wearing a pair of pink, fuzzy handcuffs, my tears instantly turning to laughter. I also remember never telling anyone about that bear—I wanted to keep that to myself as long as possible.

"It...was...you." The astonishment in my voice is palpable.

"Of course it was me," she confirms, but she sounds frustrated. I could not tell if she was still mad at me, or if she was mad at herself for revealing her role in the whole thing. "He called me and asked me if I would help with your present. Ignoring the letter for the moment, does that sound like someone who wants to be with anyone but you?"

And without having me vocalize it, Aphrodite draws the truth behind my fears from me: I am afraid not because I do not trust Prince Charming; I am afraid because I do not trust anyone currently around him.

"What if..." I begin, but Aphrodite is not going to let me run away from this.

"Did this jackass get transferred to the Beautiful Mountain?"

"Not to my knowledge—"

"No, he didn't." She was practically yelling now. "Because if he had, he wouldn't have written you a damn letter! And it doesn't matter if he gets out before Prince Charming or after Prince Charming or if they're release on the same damn day; once Prince Charming is back home, once you two are back together, this idiot is going to matter even less than he does now. And that is going to be amazing, because from what I can tell, he doesn't matter at all."

I drove in silence, the part of my brain steering the car on autopilot. Sensing that I be able to finish a complete thought, I decide to risk asking a question.

"What if he comes looking for us?"

The phone is silent, then I heard the most surprising and unexpected sound.

Aphrodite was laughing at me.

She was not chuckling; she was not even snickering. She was laughing: full-bellied, raucous laughter that echoed in the silence of the car as it sped through the night.

"I really hope he's not that stupid," she managed to fit in between chortles. "From what I heard, you and Athena made a pretty terrifying team back in the day. If something happens, I imagine you'll be able to ...handle it."

The mention of my old partner from the Navy threw me. I know that Aphrodite and Athena have never crossed paths; the latter was out of the country on business when my inner circle became acquainted. Sure, I had told some sea stories and Athena did have a reputation for intimidation. We had not worked together in twenty years and she still scared the hell out of me.

"So," I say quietly, "I'm being stupid?"

"Yes."

"And I have nothing to worry about?"

"Now, now, my dear. I didn't say that."

What the hell?

"You have tons of things to worry about, my dear," she said, her voice finally adopting that comforting tone that I had originally sought. "Your marriage just isn't one of them."

Aphrodite's advice resembled so many other things in life; sometimes you have to endure the bad in order to get to the good.

For better and for worse...

The Goddess of Love had spoken, and the weight and finality of her words silently said that this topic was over and done. We chatted about nonsensical things for a few minutes, and I soon let her return to revel with her guests. I was almost halfway through my journey to the Beautiful Mountain, and the sun would be up soon. I wanted to be headed west on I-10 before it broke over the horizon; I hated the glare it created, especially here in southern Louisiana where there was no topography to hide the blazing ball of light.

I turn onto yet another state highway and, so startled by what I see, almost steer my car directly into the roadside ditch.. In front of me is a two-story inflated snowman, lit from the inside, a banner between its branch-like hands advertising snow cones. I guide my car back to the safety of the asphalt, consciously work at slowing my breathing.

Although, after the day I have endured, a thirty-foot light-up snowman in the middle of summer should not have come as such a surprise.

I let my mind begin to wander, unbound and unrestrained. As is often the case, my brain begins to make seemingly-random connections which, once revealed, are laughably obvious in their simplicity.

The memory of a high-school English paper on one of Andersen's lesser-known fairy tales swims to the front of my mind and I swear that in the distance I can hear the Universe chuckling at its own cleverness.

It was on New Year's Eve in 1860 when Hans Christian Andersen allegedly penned a fairy tale full of passionate and undying love, and separation, angst, and despair. True to form, Andersen ends the tale not with the joyous union of two lovers, but with his usual motif of love and passion unrequited.

Then again, this is a tale where a snowman falls in love with a stove. In comparison, "The Little Mermaid" reads almost like a documentary.

Many biographers have speculated that Andersen's infatuation with a male ballet dancer twenty years his junior served as the inspiration for this tale of woe, though we may never truly know if this is, in fact, the case.

In "The Snowman," the titular character is an actual snowman, constructed one winter's day in the garden of a fine estate. On the first day of his existence in his idyllic paradise, he can hear the jingle of sleigh bells, the laughter of children, and the crack of a whip on a horse's back. Beside him, there is an old dog on a chain, his aged voice so hoarse he can not even bark properly.

This fact, however, does not seem to prevent the dog from talking, sometimes incessantly.

The snowman asks the dog about the sun, and the dog

warns him that one day soon, it would make the snowman melt and run into the ditch. As the sun climbs higher in the sky, the snowman loses all concern, for he feels that he can be better admired now that he is properly lit.

A pair of lovers pass, and the dog talks of how he never bites either of them: the man is fond of stroking his back and the woman occasionally slips him bits of meat.

Soon, the dog is reveling in the memories of his younger days—when he slept beneath the stove which sat in the housekeeper's room on the first floor. Today, the doors to that room are open wide, and as the snowman looks upon the squat, black stove, he instantly feels something strange come over him—he feels as if he has fallen in love.

He asks the dog how he came to be chained up outside, but does not even wait to listen to the response. He is now wholly fixated on the object of his attraction. Twilight falls, and the snowman's obsession grows, so much so that when the grate on the stove was opened and flames leapt out as a result, he felt as if the stove had flicked her tongue out at him, teasing him, inviting him, enticing him.

The stove had done no such thing, except that which it was made to do.

It was, after all, a stove.

On the first night of his existence, when the stove went dark, the snowman did not despair, for he had his own reflection to admire in the panes of the windows.

But when morning came, those panes were frosted over with lacy flowers of ice and the stove was hidden from view. Despite the beauty of the ice flowers, the snowman rapidly became ill, pining away for the stove, for on this day, it was so cold that the ice did not melt from the panes.

This day—according to the overly-talkative dog—was a proper winter's day for the snowman, a day which was full of cold and whipped by wind. The dog encouraged the snowman to enjoy the time which lay wasting before him, for soon the weather would change and, when that happened, it would be the snowman who would be wasting away.

But the snowman could not be consoled, and he spent the entire second day of his existence staring at the ice flowers on the windows, desperate to see the stove within.

But change the weather did.

On the third—and final—day of his existence, the warmth increased while the snowman decreased, slowly melting from the now-dripping tableau of a winter wonderland. As he withered, the snow man did not speak nor did he complain, for the rake which he had used as a mouth was one of the first pieces to fall to the soggy earth.

Not even the dog noticed when the snowman finally fell away completely, leaving behind the hard, black iron of the stove poker, which the boys of the house had used to form the snowman's backbone.

"Well, that explains it," said the dog, now to no one, explaining to nobody that the poker belonged not in the yard, but next to the stove, in the warmth of the home.

Winter drew to a close, and before long the garden was lush and green, and while the girls of the house sang, and the dog in the yard barked, no one thought any more of the Snow Man.

When the sun explodes over the horizon behind me, I am already speeding west on I-10, having already left Louisiana and the gargantuan snowman behind me. The Beautiful Mountain is still an hour away, but the blinding light reflected in the rear-view mirror snaps me out of my meditation on the love life of a man who died nearly a century and a half ago.

The anger which I had consumed me since the moment I read the Dutchman's letter still simmers inside me, and as I draw closer to my destination, it now threatens to boil over and transform into a primal, seething rage. My brain can easily understand Aphrodite's explanation: the fury my heart feels is nothing more than fear's cowardly mask. That knowledge, however, cannot shift my heart's perception of the situation.

One of the oft-misunderstood benefits of an existence absent from strong emotions is the ability to apply logic a situation—any situation—and be almost instantly rewarded with a solution built upon a strong, stable footing which would endure even the most detailed scrutiny without fail.

The logic of my current quandary had been helpfully pointed out by Aphrodite: this errant suitor is—and would always be—nearly nothing in the fate-filled tapestry of my life. Prince Charming is the one who had to endure the longing stares and the inappropriate notes, one of which I still possessed in a box along with everything else Charming had sent home from the Tower in Elmdingle.

Taken together, all those facts should have soothed my soul, but my heart remains troubled. I know that fear is often irrational, but I also know it exists for a reason: it is a primal urge that we feel upon sensing danger, either to ourselves or someone, or something, that we love.

The clarity which breaks through into my mind is nearly as spectacular as the dawn which had broken across the lowland landscape not long ago. I am not galloping toward Prince Charming's Tower for answers.

I no longer have any questions.

It may have taken a day of wallowing in self-pity, dinner with my Mother, a slight lack of sleep, an early-morning berating one of my best friends, and almost three hours of solitude in the car as I drove through two states, but now I understand why the Dutchman chose to write to me, desperate for knowledge of Prince Charming.

The Dutchman is nothing more than a Snow Man.

To me, Prince Charming had always glowed with a brilliance of which even he may not have been aware. He is possessed of a liquid personality, one which fills whatever space he happens to be occupying, whether it is our den, a cell in a Tower, or my heart. His natural intuition is so finely-tuned that it borders on precognition; I learned very early in our relationship to trust it, especially if the voices of my past would protest its contradiction to their long-held and time-honored beliefs.

One of my coworkers, Gabriel, often quoted a line he pulled from a wall poster somewhere in his past: "Just because you've always done it that way doesn't mean it's not stupid."

During the days before Prince Charming, I lived in a perpetual state of fear that simply being me would not be good enough for my chosen partner. Whether by fate or self-fulfilling prophecy, a breakup would always come to pass.

Gabriel may have had a point, and when Prince Charming came along, I took a different path.

He never asked me to be anything but myself, nor did he set standards that I had to attain in order to keep his affection.

He tore down my masks and my shields while simultaneously dropping his own, revealing that flawed perfection that the thought of its beauty—even now—still makes my breath catch in my throat.

Prince Charming blazes like a stove that has been properly fed: a steady but brilliant glow which affects everyone with whom he comes into contact. The warmth may not last forever, but there is absolutely no doubt that the fire was there.

The Dutchman never stood a chance.

Like Andersen's stove which was hidden from the Snow Man, Prince Charming has now been hidden away from the Dutchman—forever. And like the Snow Man in the fairy tale, soon the memory of the Dutchman will melt and run off into a ditch, just like my car almost did when I saw a two-story snowman lit up on the side of the road.

PART FOUR
THE SPRING

As I pull into the parking lot of the Tower, I am happy to see that only a few people have lined up in the visitors queue. I open the glove box and take one of the plastic bags partially filled with loose quarters which I keep there should I spontaneously choose to make a trip to Charming's Tower.

After all, it does not require a letter from a sociopath to make me want to see my husband.

I line up dutifully behind those visitors already here, my mind clear, trying to figure out precisely how I will explain my surprise appearance to Prince Charming. I briefly consider leaving the letter out altogether, but quickly dismiss the thought as I remember my oath to always tell him when I am in distress. He may not be able to hold me with his arms, but I have learned to find the same level of comfort in the simple sound of his voice.

After only an hour and a half—quite possibly a new record—I am processed through the front of the Tower, and once in the visiting room I make directly for the vending machines on the far wall. I spend almost fifteen full dollars on candy, junk food and other snacks, holding the remaining money in reserve should we desire something a bit more substantial later.

If my Mother had borne witness to this seemingly-frivolous spending spree, she would have most likely become apoplectic. However, Prince Charming regularly ate candy for breakfast before he was taken away; I see no need to stop him now. Besides, the Dowager Queen and I maintain a running wager on his A1C number—the primary indicator of how close a person is to developing diabetes.

Gathering up the sugary goods, I find a chair away from the small but growing crowd, hopeful for a spot of partial privacy. I dump the snacks into the seat beside me, and immediately indulge my neurotic, nervous habit of lining up the corners of the candy bars, and arranging the whole pile into something that appears to have square corners and equal sides. I think of all the hours I spent playing Tetris when I was younger, and am grateful to finally have another real-world application for those skills; my ability to load a dishwasher is already off the charts.

"Baby?"

The sound of Charming's voice—transmitted through the air and not across a telephone line—stops the motion of my hands cold, and I exercise all restraint possible as I turn and smile brightly at him. His blue eyes are confused and he is scanning me for any sign of injury or harm.

Finding none, he swings his eyes back up, but I am already on my feet, moving in for our allotted quick hug. Throwing caution to the wind, I plant a quick kiss on his lips, grateful that there are not many observers around, since we have never tried this before out of fear.

I am utterly amazed when I realize that no one in the room gives a damn.

I start tossing candy at Charming, filling him in on the past twenty-four hours and the real reason for my journey: I wanted to see him and I wanted him to see me.

His hands clench when I speak of the Dutchman's words and it is almost an hour before his breathing returns to normal. As usual, we break up the heavier conversation topics with lighter ones, sometimes descending into outright gossip about our friends and members of our family. Gossip might be the lowest form of discourse, but in the visiting room of a prison, one cannot afford to be picky.

The room is filling to capacity now, but today is not one of our generous days; today we will take however long we are allowed, and not a moment less. When I lean forward, he does the same, both of us with our hands on our knees. I can see his wedding ring in stark contrast to his pale skin—despite his overall appearance of well-being, he obviously has been avoiding the heat by staying indoors. But as my eyes focus on the cobalt-blue band, I feel as if I am being pulled forward into its depths, and the scene before me shifts suddenly.

At our wedding, when we sealed our union, I saw infinity laid bare before me, and it is this never-ending hallway in which I again find myself. Although I know I have not moved from my seat in the visitor's room, I can now look to the past and see the same couples I first beheld on my wedding day.

Now, however, those who came before Prince Charming and I look drastically different.

The couple in Victorian garb look deathly pale, and one of them is coughing into a handkerchief which seems to get redder with each expectoration. The medieval couple are still working in the same field, but the harvest is poor, and I can see that they are malnourished.

The most terrifying scene lies just inside my field of vision: the Librarian and the Soldier. The Librarian's robes are obviously singed, and even smoldering in some places. He cradles the Soldier in his arms, his mouth moving quickly as he offers reassurance to his partner, whose wound appears to be nothing short of mortal.

The horror of the scene barely has time to register before I am yanked back into the visiting room, most likely by Prince Charming's silent wish.

Even across hundreds of miles—and now apparently the continuum of space and time—I know when he is thinking of me.

I see the fear in his eyes, and I assure him that I am okay, only for him to realize that he has been eating all the snacks and I have been letting him.

A chocolate bar lands in my lap and a monosyllabic command is uttered: "Eat."

I open my mouth to protest, but a single raised eyebrow silences me and I begin to unwrap the candy bar. I muse silently on whether or not to tell Prince Charming that he just perfectly executed one of his mother-in-law's signature moves, but decide against it.

In all honesty, I would rather tell Atropos first.

Weeks later, it is a late summer Saturday, and for once I am not at the Beautiful Mountain visiting my Prince. I am helping with a book drive at the local public library, which I was shocked to discover was only one block away from my loft. I am only here for a day, and people are coming in and out, some with donations and some without, simply stopping by to pick up something to read.

"JOHNNY, I SAID SLOW DOWN!"

As I hear the shout, I realize that I know the voice and the person to whom it belongs has no issue with yelling in a library. In all honesty, she would probably yell at a funeral.

I turn and see Marla, my letter carrier, coming through the glass double doors preceded by at least four children of varying ages. One boy—who I can only assume is Johnny—is quickly pulling ahead of the pack, making a beeline for the young adult fiction section. Marla instructs each of her charges in turn, sending them off in different directions before exhaling a huge breath and turning to go about her own business in the library.

When she sees me, she stops cold. She looks back over her shoulder, then back at me. She makes a production of turning in a full circle, looking up and down the walls, before walking up to me and grabbing my hand.

"Well then," she says. "You're real. Are you lost?"

"No," I say, a laugh already forming in the back of my throat.

"But this is the library and not your apartment. Am I lost?"

"No, Marla, neither one of us is lost," I answer. "I heard they needed help, so I came down to help. Everything at my place is packed up, so there's not much to do there."

"Uh-huh," she says, still looking at me as if I might disappear at any moment. "I got your change of address notice, so I figured you'd be moving soon. I guess I'll have to go back to not talking to anybody during my day."

I am stunned. I had assumed that I was just another face to Marla. I did not realize my departure would affect her at all.

"Although, if I'm being honest, and I always am," she says, "I'd been expecting that form for a while. Although, the forwarding address did surprise me. I thought for sure you would be moving to the Beautiful Mountain."

"So did I," I agreed, "but something changed. It turns out my job isn't to follow him all over the country."

"Really? Then what is your job?"

"Oh, that's easy," I reply. "It's my job to keep the light lit at the end of the tunnel."

"But why all the way up there? You do know it gets cold up there, right? You got family there?"

"No, ma'am, no family that far north. I thought about what you said about LSU, and it turns out that there's a perfectly-good college right there in town."

"What school?"

"Ashing College," I say. "And don't worry, I don't even think they have a football team. I'll get to keep my garnet-and-gold, at least on Saturdays in the fall."

"You gonna be all alone up there? I mean, you were alone here, but at least I came by once a week to make sure you were still alive."

My guilt over my departure deepens. If Marla has picked up on it, she doesn't give a sign that she notices or even cares. She stares calmly at me waiting for an answer.

"One of my best friends is helping me fix up the place and she will probably stay for...well, I don't know. But it will be a while."

"Where's she from?" Marla asks.

"Atlanta, but she grew up in Miami," I reply.

"MIAMI! Aw, no," says Marla, shaking her head back and forth. "We gonna have to pray for her; she might not make it through winter."

"I'll buy her a long coat," I say, amused.

"You do that. Does she mind leaving the house occasionally and actually interacting with other people?"

"You could say she does it professionally."

I suddenly realize that I might have accidentally told Marla that Artemis was a prostitute and not a bartender.

"Well, let me go round up those kids. They should be okay, I can't smell any smoke." Marla waves at me as she wanders off, another one of her million-watt smiles thrown over her shoulder for good measure.

I stand very still for several minutes, thinking about the friend I had unknowingly made here in Louisiana, one whose worth I did not realize until this very day. When I feel a finger tap me on the shoulder, I gasp and spin around.

I'm staring into deep gray eyes set in a face of pure beauty. The woman's dark brown hair rolls in waves off the back of her head and she is dressed in a white button up shirt and slacks.

A gold pendant lays against her neck, but I cannot quite make out what it is supposed to be.

"Did you hear me?" she asks, concern in her eyes. "I asked if you are the librarian."

"Um, no, " I stumble. "She's over there behind the round desk." I point toward a woman in her early twenties sitting bored behind a desk which dwarfs her diminutive frame. The gray-eyed woman keeps her eyes on me and I turn back, suddenly aware of her gaze.

"Very well," she says, turning to head across the room. "You just looked like you would be a librarian in Alexandria."

EPILOGUE

Once again, the white paint on my car seems to glow in the twilight as it races along a quiet stretch of U.S. Highway 23 in North Carolina. Unlike my odyssey to Alexandria, the setting sun is behind me, not before me, dappling the landscape with purples and blues and other muted colors. To my left, the majestic mountains of the Blue Ridge rise sharply, their summits out of sight, their sides sheer.

While my goal—to live out my days with Prince Charming—remains unchanged, the path my journey will take has shifted. I am not headed to the Tower on the Beautiful Mountain; I am no longer headed to a town with a Tower at all.

I am headed to the Castle.

On the Eastern Shore of the Chesapeake Bay there sits a house, a house that has stood longer than almost every single building in the city of Atlanta. The peaked roof, hardwood floors, pocket doors, and secret staircase were built in a time when life was less complicated, less congested, and less connected. The keyhole in the red front door is shaped—at least to my eyes—precisely how a keyhole should be shaped: the merging of a circle atop a triangle. For over a hundred years the Castle has weathered the tide and the time in its bucolic setting, and while the paint is peeling and there is a crack or two in the plaster walls, the bones of the house are strong, and the foundation is solid.

The stalwart structure of the Castle reflects my marriage to Prince Charming: not without its battle scars and blemishes, but with a structure and a footing that will ensure it endures the test of time.

"'Til death," was the phrase used at our wedding. Death—not distance, not despair, not even district attorneys.

And—most certainly—not the Dutchman.

Once again, the Universe has shown Prince Charming and me our path, but allowed us the choice in whether or not to take it. After the events of the past year, we did not hesitate for a moment.

There is a subtle movement on my right, and I spare a quick look to my companion. Artemis' long legs shift in her sleep, and she is lying as flat as possible in the somewhat confining space of the car. She faces me, smiling gently in her sleep. I had told her about the Castle and before I could even ask for help fixing the place up, it had been offered.

After all, without Bonnie, who is Clyde, really?

The city of Charlotte is still an hour away, and I am tempted to speed through the Queen City instead of stopping and letting Artemis drive the next few hours as we had agreed.

Then again, I have no wish to be on the receiving end of

her loving wrath while in a confined space.

I reach over and grab her shoulder, gently shaking her awake. Her eyes remain shut, her hand reaching up and settling over my own, the ever-present warmth of her skin noticeable even in the heat of a midsummer night in the American South.

"Are we in Charlotte yet?" she asks, her voice pitched high, and if I'm being honest, a bit nasal.

"Not yet," I reply, putting my hand back on the wheel. Artemis sits up, then adjusts the seat so it now supports her back.

"Then why did you wake me up?" she mutters.

"I thought you might like to see this," I say simply, pointing through the windshield.

The last glimmer of daylight dies behind us, but in the moment before it is gone, the steep but gentle slopes of the mountain are awash in muted jewel tones of color, with only the inky backdrop of night behind them, before they fade completely to black, where the only difference between the mountains and the night sky is the presence of stars.

"This is going to be amazing," Artemis says, leaning her long body forward so she can see through the top of the windshield. "What are you going to do when it snows?"

I am silent for a moment. Annual snowfall was practically a guarantee in Maryland, despite the warmth of the currents that surround the Chesapeake Bay.

Then I remember the delight in Prince Charming's eyes every year when the snow would fall in Atlanta, even if it was a light dusting whose only accomplishment was to force traffic to grind to a halt. Through the back door he would dash—no coat, no hat, no gloves—and run around like a child who had never beheld frozen precipitation before.

The memory makes me smile, and my answer is subtly simple.

"I think," I say, "we will build a snowman."

THE END

ABOUT THE AUTHOR

Zachary A. Calais—born and raised in Atlanta, Georgia—spent decades working in a variety of industries (including hospitality, information technology, project management, graphic design and copy writing.) It was during these years—usually stuck in airports and hotel rooms while traveling for business—that he began penning short stories as a cure for boredom. These stories would eventually form the base of his first collection: *Observations from a Third-Story Window and Other Stories.*

Zachary is currently developing several works, including the *The Mistress of Passion* and *Something Redneck This Way Comes*—a further examination of one of the most-beloved characters from his first book: Big Red.

He is married to Eric Lee Calais, and resides with his growing family in the Atlanta area, despite multiple attempts to leave the city forever.

COMING IN FALL 2017

MY LIFE AS A FAIRY TALE

THE BEGINNING

This new edition collects together Calais' previously-published fairy-tale allegories, including "Rapunzel" to "The Little Mermaid" and every story in between.

The book will also include Mr. Calais' unreleased "My Life as a Fairy Tale: Pinocchio", which details the Narrator's initial descent into despair following Charming's incarceration, and of his odyssey from Atlanta to the bayou of Western Louisiana.

COMING SOON

The Atlanta Series
The Ascent of Icarus

In the third installment of Zachary Calais' *Atlanta Series*, The Narrator has left the long shadow of the Tower behind as he prepares a new home and a new life in anticipation of Prince Charming's release from incarceration.

But what happens when a new player appears on the board—a friend who sees through the Narrator's pain without effort—rekindling the fiery passion once thought lost within the Narrator's broken soul?

Will this new protegé drive the Narrator toward a fuller life—one which is worth living, or together will they fly too close to the sun? Will they be able to tell the difference?

The Saga of Big Red
Something Redneck this way Comes

In the first volume completely dedicated to the redneck un-beauty queen, Calais uses a unique storytelling technique in order to remain true to the oral tradition begun in *The Ballad of Big Red*. Various speakers recount the tale of their experiences with the woman who firmly believed, and practiced daily that the higher the hair, the closer to God.